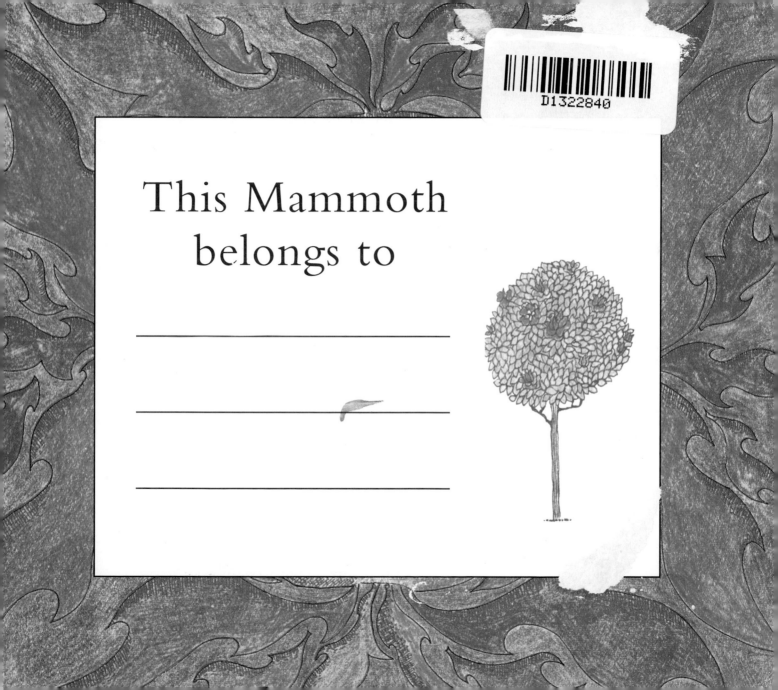

This Mammoth belongs to

_____

_____

_____

D1322840

Picture Mammoths
illustrated by Helen Oxenbury

Pig Tale

**The Helen Oxenbury
Nursery Story Book**

**The Helen Oxenbury
Nursery Rhyme Book**
Rhymes chosen by Brian Alderson

**The Three Little Wolves
and the Big Bad Pig**
Text by Eugene Trivizas

Tiny Tim
*Verses for children
chosen by Jill Bennett*

The Quangle Wangle's Hat
Poem by Edward Lear

The Great Big Enormous Turnip

PICTURES BY
Helen Oxenbury

STORY BY
Alexei Tolstoy

689427
MORAY COUNCIL
DEPARTMENT OF TECHNICAL
& LEISURE SERVICES
JA

First published in Great Britain 1968
by William Heinemann Ltd
Published 1998 by Mammoth
an imprint of Reed International Books Limited
Michelin House, 81 Fulham Road, London SW3 6RB

10 8 6 4 2 1 3 5 7 9

Illustrations copyright © Helen Oxenbury 1968
Helen Oxenbury has asserted her moral rights

ISBN 0 7497 2405 6

A CIP catalogue record for this title
is available from the British Library

Printed in Hong Kong by Wing King Tong Co. Ltd.

This paperback is sold subject to the condition
that it shall not, by way of trade or otherwise, be lent,
resold, hired out, or otherwise circulated without the publisher's
prior consent in any form of binding or cover other than that
in which it is published and without a similar condition including
this condition being imposed on the subsequent purchaser.

Once upon a time an old man planted
a little turnip and said,
"Grow, grow, little turnip, grow sweet. Grow,
grow, little turnip, grow strong."

And the turnip grew up sweet and strong,
and big and enormous.
Then, one day, the old man went to
pull it up.
He pulled and pulled again, but he could
not pull it up.

He called the old woman.

The old woman pulled the old man.
The old man pulled the turnip.
And they pulled and pulled again, but they
could not pull it up.

So the old woman called her granddaughter.

The granddaughter pulled the old woman,
The old woman pulled the old man,
The old man pulled the turnip.
And they pulled and pulled again, but they
could not pull it up.

The granddaughter called
the black dog.

The black dog pulled the granddaughter,
The granddaughter pulled the old woman,
The old woman pulled the old man,
The old man pulled the turnip.
And they pulled and pulled again, but they
could not pull it up.

The black dog called the cat.

The cat pulled the dog.
The dog pulled the granddaughter,
The granddaughter pulled the old woman,
The old woman pulled the old man,
The old man pulled the turnip.
And they pulled and pulled again, but still they could not pull it up.

The cat called the mouse.

The mouse pulled the cat,
The cat pulled the dog,
The dog pulled the granddaughter,
The granddaughter pulled the old woman,
The old woman pulled the old man,
The old man pulled the turnip.

They pulled and pulled again, and up came the turnip at last.